ANGELS ON ROLLER SKATES

"Middlun," Mom called, *"where on earth are you?"*
"Holding the ladder for you," said a small voice beneath.

ANGELS ON ROLLER SKATES

written and illustrated by
MAGGIE HARRISON

CANDLEWICK PRESS
CAMBRIDGE, MASSACHUSETTS

For my Bigun, both Middluns, and Littlun

First U.S. edition 1992
First published in Great Britain in 1990 by
Walker Books Ltd., London.
ISBN 1-56402-003-7
Library of Congress Catalog Card Number 91-71862
Library of Congress Cataloging-in-Publication information
is available.

10 9 8 7 6 5 4 3 2 1
Printed in the United States

Candlewick Press
2067 Massachusetts Avenue
Cambridge, Massachusetts 02140

CONTENTS

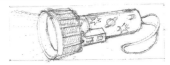

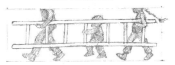

When you had feet as big as Bigun's,
you didn't look like an infant.

THE BICYCLE
AND THE
SWIMMING CAP

Bigun was big for his age and proud of it. Middlun was smaller, but she had an extra long braid to make up for it. Littlun was smallest of all. He got in everybody's way when he was crawling and got on everyone's nerves when he was yelling.

Bigun went to Church Lane Primary School nearby. He was proud of that too, because Middlun was not quite old enough to go to school yet. The only thing he hated about school was having to go in a door that had "Infants" carved in big stone letters above it. When you had feet as big as Bigun's, you didn't look like an infant, and Bigun certainly didn't feel like one.

The family lived in an apartment above a restaurant in a row of small stores. Their restaurant was called Biggerburger, and it sold take-out burgers—beefburgers, cheeseburgers, eggburgers, onionburgers, and veggieburgers. The children were not allowed in the shop while their father was working, so they stayed upstairs with their mother or went for walks to the playground or along the towpath by the canal. Littlun had to go in a stroller because he couldn't walk yet, but Mom kept Middlun's old reins, because she said he would be needing them any minute now.

In November, Bigun was seven, and his best present of all was a bicycle. It was not a BMX bike, because Dad said he didn't want Bigun breaking his neck, but it was a big one and it looked like a racing bike. Dad took him to the store to choose it three days before his birthday. During those three days Bigun dreamed of riding his bike to school and skimming across the playground to the bicycle stands. He imagined the admiration and envy of the other children as he arrived in a blur of scarlet and silver, and how people would scatter as he rang his bell.

Only it didn't happen that way. On his birthday Bigun discovered that he couldn't actually ride his bicycle without his father holding the seat. It was harder than it looked. He tried again and again, but every time he shouted to his dad to let go, he wobbled and fell off. Bigun began to get really angry with himself, but his parents only laughed and said, "You'll soon get the hang of it. It's only a question of keeping your balance. By next week, you'll be fine."

"Huh," thought Bigun, "that sounds like waiting for Littlun to walk!" His dream of riding through the school gates faded, and he glared at his shiny new bicycle. He had told everybody about it and how he would bring it to school on Monday.

"Well, you could always wheel it there and show it to everyone," Dad suggested. Bigun gave him a shriveling look and decided to say he had a flat tire if anyone asked where it was—just until he got the hang of it.

Middlun said, "Can I try? I'm sure I could ride it."

Bigun glared at her. He was sure *she* would be able to, but not before him!

"Don't you dare touch my bicycle while I'm at school. If you even put one foot on a pedal, I'll . . . I'll cut all your hair off while you're asleep! I mean it."

He zipped up his jacket and walked to school.

Middlun spent most of the morning playing in the hallway, looking longingly at the bicycle. It was so shiny. Even the red parts were shinier than anything she had ever seen before. She stroked the handlebars and felt the smooth chill of new chrome. The handlebar grips fitted her hands exactly. She listened, holding her breath. Upstairs her mother was feeding Littlun and watching a program on child development. Through the wall to her right was the restaurant, and she could hear her father taking a lunch order from one of the builders at the yard.

"So that's four cheese with ketchup, two beef with and one without, and three onion with hamburger relish."

Middlun quietly opened the front door, and quietly wheeled the bicycle outside.

At first she just walked up and down the sidewalk outside the other stores, wheeling it proudly. Then, as the streets emptied during lunch hour, she thought she would just see if the seat felt right. It did, but her toes only just touched the ground on each side if she stretched very hard. She knew she could ride it, but she also knew that Bigun could easily cut her hair off in the night with the kitchen scissors. So she left the pedals alone and paddled herself along using the tips of her toes. This was fun and quite easy. You couldn't fall over with both of your feet on the ground. She went a little faster, then rounded the corner. It was getting easier and easier.

The road sloped down toward the canal. It was not a steep hill, just a gentle slope, and Middlun didn't have to use her feet to push herself along anymore. She sailed down with both legs sticking right out. She wasn't touching the pedals, which were whirring around by themselves, but she *was* riding the bicycle, which was more than Bigun could do!

She stopped on the grass at the bottom of the hill and then turned back onto the sidewalk, pushing the bike all the way up the slope to have another ride down. This time it was even faster and even better. And instead of looking down at the sidewalk, she looked up

*Middlun sailed down with both
legs sticking right out.*

proudly, hoping that someone would see her. And someone did.

Along the towpath on the other side of the canal, a class of children was collecting leaves. And there was Bigun, staring at her with absolute fury, a bunch of leaves crumpled in his clenched fist. Middlun came to a careful stop, thankful that the water was between them. She turned the bike around and wheeled it home as fast as she could. Her mother was standing outside the restaurant, with Littlun on her hip, looking anxiously up and down the street.

"Middlun, how dare you take that bike out without asking! You can't ride it anyway—even Bigun can't. If you wanted to wheel it up and down, you should have asked him first. Now get it inside, and put it back exactly where you found it."

Middlun did, then slunk upstairs. When Bigun came home from school, she said quickly, "I didn't touch a single pedal. Not once. Anyway, it's easier to balance if you don't bother with the pedals."

Bigun ate his dinner in silence and left his sister watching TV. He took his bicycle outside, down the slope toward the canal—several times. And then a few more times.

Just before Dad opened the restaurant for the evening, Bigun said, "Come out and watch me, Dad, just for a minute."

Dad came to the door and watched, as Bigun slowly and carefully pedaled past.

"Well done, Bigun! My goodness, you learn fast. How did you pick up the trick of balancing?"

"It's easy," said Bigun, carefully concentrating, with a big grin that almost reached his ears.

But that night Middlun slept badly. Under her pillow she had hidden five pairs of scissors—the big kitchen ones, Mom's pinking

*Under her pillow, Middlun had
hidden five pairs of scissors.*

shears, a pair of nail scissors, the little embroidery ones, and even the blunt round-ended pair that she was allowed to use for cutting out paper. You couldn't be too careful with brothers around.

Her mother had no idea why her daughter had gone to sleep wearing a blue-and-white flowered swimming cap.

Bigun whispered out of the corner of
his mouth, "Want to join the Club?"

THE CLUB

Bigun came home from school looking important. He ate his dinner with a little smile on his face, in silence. Middlun decided not to ask him what was the matter. It was quicker that way. Under cover of watching TV, Bigun whispered out of the corner of his mouth, "Want to join the Club?"

"Yes," said Middlun. She was always joining in at playgroup, so she knew about joining things. Then she asked, "What's the Club?"

"It's mine, and I'm the leader."

"But where is it and what do you do with it?" Middlun was looking at her brother's pockets hopefully.

"It's some people, all together, and they

21

meet in a secret place and have a code and do secret interesting things. You'll find out how it works once you've joined. And it costs half a Snickers to join. You've got one in the kitchen cabinet."

"All right," said Middlun agreeably, having eaten it after lunch. "Who else is in the Club and where do we meet?"

"Well, I thought we'd start off with just us to begin with, and when it's working, we'll ask somebody else."

"Not Littlun. He's too young."

"Of course not Littlun. He'd be useless. Maybe Jarvis or Daniel. We'll see. But we've got to find a secret place to meet. Somewhere we won't be disturbed. That's difficult."

"No it isn't," said Middlun quickly. "The bathroom."

"Don't be stupid. You can't have a club in the bathroom."

"Why not? It's the only place I know where

you don't get disturbed, and it's the only room that locks."

"All right, it can be the bathroom for the moment. Then we'll find somewhere else. Now, we need some paper and a pencil to write the rules, and we should take something to eat because that's what clubs do. I'll get the paper, you get something to eat, and we'll meet in two minutes."

Middlun didn't know how long two minutes was, but she guessed it wasn't long. *Two* wasn't a big number of anything, except elephants or buses. Anyway, Bigun only had to get his knapsack for the paper. She wandered into the kitchen where her mother was slicing onions for supper, screwing up her eyes to stop them from watering. Littlun was investigating an eggbeater under the table. Middlun took a carrot and a cooking apple from the table while her mother was trying to wipe her eyes on the inside of an elbow, and then

*Middlun took a carrot and a cooking
apple from the table.*

she joined Bigun in the bathroom. It was a long, narrow room with a window at one end above the toilet and a row of boots at the other end.

Bigun was already sitting on the lid of the toilet seat with a notebook on his lap and a marker in his hand, all ready to write. Middlun bolted the door firmly and made a pile of boots to sit on. She put the carrot and the apple inside one of the boots, a small red one of Littlun's.

"The first thing to decide on is a name. We've got to be the something Club," said Bigun.

"All right," said Middlun happily, "the *Something* Club sounds very secret because nobody knows what the *Something* is."

Bigun gave up. She was too young, but he'd think of a better name later. Meanwhile, he laboriously wrote the name on the top of the paper. It slipped, so he knelt up on the seat, turning around to use the top of the tank as a desk.

Rule 1. I am Leader.

Rule 2. Meetings are secret, on Tuesdays and Fridays, in here.

Rule 3. Bring something to eat.

Rule 4. Decide things.

"What things?" asked Middlun.

"Oh, what we're going to do next time."

"What are we going to do now?"

"Break the carrot in half and eat it."

Bigun would never have believed carrots could be so hard to break. In the end, he bit it and gave half to Middlun, who settled herself comfortably on the boots to eat it.

Just then the door handle turned.

"Sorry," they heard Mom say, "didn't know anyone was inside."

"Won't be a minute," called Bigun indistinctly, through a mouthful of carrot. He slipped off the seat and flushed the toilet.

"Go on out," he whispered to Middlun. "Mom'll be back in a minute. Then afterward, we'll come back and write down some more rules."

Middlun quickly put the boots in a row and went to the door.

"I can't undo the bolt," she said after a brief struggle.

"Let me, silly. You're probably pulling it the wrong way."

"I am not. It's stuck."

Mom tried the handle again, and then she knocked.

"Hurry up, Bigun. Don't take all day in there."

"No, Mom, I'll be out in a minute." Elbowing Middlun out of the way, he looked at the bolt. There was a little knob on top of the handle, a very small one, and Middlun had pushed it flat against the door when she'd bolted it. He scrabbled with his fingers but couldn't move it at all.

"We've got to lift it up as far as here, and then we can slide it back." He tried pressure from each side in turn, but it didn't even wobble.

They both heard Mom calling Middlun.

Middlun didn't dare answer. They looked at each other.

"What on earth did you do to it?"

"I just pushed it, that's all. I've done it lots of times with the door open. Mom said not to play with it when the door was closed in case I got locked in, and . . ." She stopped and looked at Bigun. "And Mom wouldn't be able to get me out because you can't open the window like an ordinary one." Her voice wavered, and her mouth and chin began to wobble. Bigun felt furious with her, with the stupid bolt, and with himself. There was no point in looking at the window. It wouldn't open because it was a new one that Dad had specially fitted with clever slats of glass that let in air but nothing else.

There was a deadly silence. Middlun was waiting for her brother to have an idea before she cried. If it was a good one, she wouldn't, but if it was a bad one, she would fill the little room with her crying.

They heard Mom's footsteps. She tried the door handle. "Bigun, you're not *still* in there! Come out quickly. I'm in a hurry. I've left Littlun in a kitchen cabinet, and I can't find Middlun. What's the matter with you?" The door handle turned and twisted and rattled.

"Sorry, Mom," Bigun's voice sounded really small. "The bolt's stuck, and I can't get out. And Middlun's in here with me."

"I can't bear it," said Mom flatly. "I've asked your dad a thousand times to move that bolt or make a better lock. Just hang on while I put Littlun in the playpen, and then I'll think of something." They could hear her running back to the kitchen, and Littlun screaming as he was deprived of a whole collection of pans. Then she came back.

"If I can slide a wrench through the window slats, could you knock the bolt free? I can't get Dad. He's just opened up, and there's a line a mile long. Wait a minute while I find the ladder. When I tap on the glass, pull the long cord to open the slats, and I'll pass the wrench through. But don't let it drop, or it'll crack the tank. You'll have to stand on the toilet seat, Bigun, only put the lid down first."

Bigun was about to say, "I'm not stupid, Mom," but changed his mind.

The wrench didn't work, although they both tried with Mom calling through the door and Littlun shaking the bars of the playpen and yelling bloody murder in the kitchen. All they managed to do was to dent the wood around the bolt.

During a lull, when there were no customers, Dad ran upstairs to find out what all the noise was about.

"Honestly!" he exploded. "I am *not* going to break that window. It was a very expensive one, and it took me a long time to put it in. Bigun watched me, so he knows how long it took. As far as I'm concerned, they can stay there all night. Feed them peanuts through the keyhole if they're hungry. Oh, there isn't a keyhole? Too bad. That'll teach them not to play with bolts." And he ran down to the restaurant again.

Middlun began to howl, then stopped suddenly. "Bigun, you helped Dad put in the window, didn't you?"

"Well, almost," admitted Bigun. "I handed him the screws and helped hold the frame in place, and . . . oh, I see what you mean. Yes, the screws are on the inside. If I could unscrew them, we could take the whole window frame out and climb through the hole and down the ladder."

He called through the wall.

"Mom, could you bring a screwdriver? Then I could take the window out. I think I know how to do it."

"Thank God for that," breathed Mom, "only Middlun will have to help lift it down. Dad'll have you for supper if you break it." She raided Dad's toolbox and passed a collection of tools one by one through the glass slats. Middlun arranged them in a row on the floor.

It was very difficult to get the screws to move at all. Mom left them to do it and went to feed Littlun. Bigun struggled with the screwdriver until he felt as if his wrists were breaking. Dad had certainly done a good job of tightening them. Middlun waited to be helpful, playing with the tools.

At last Bigun said, "That's it, they're almost free. Now, Middlun, climb up here next to me and hold the bottom of the frame. Here, don't drop it." He took out the screws, one by one, and began easing the window out of the frame, holding the top carefully. Then they lowered it to the floor.

"Mom," he called, "we're coming out." So Mom ran outside to hold the bottom of the ladder. Bigun climbed onto the tank, then through the window opening, and carefully down the ladder. "I'll go around and tell Dad I got the frame out all right. Back in a minute." He ran around to the restaurant, and Mom called up to Middlun, "Your turn now, dear. It's easy. Just climb onto the toilet seat, then the tank, then one leg over the windowsill onto the ladder, and there you are." But nothing happened. Mom looked up. The window frame was quite empty.

"Oh, come on, Middlun, we can't wait all day, and it's beginning to get dark. Don't you want any supper? It's easy enough to climb down, and you're big enough to do it. It's not

Bigun climbed onto the tank,
then through the window opening.

even very far up." There was no reply and no sign of Middlun at the window.

"For goodness' sake, Middlun, you are impossible," said Mom, getting annoyed, and she began to climb the ladder herself. When she got to the top and looked in, the bathroom was empty, and the door was wide open, with the claw of a hammer hanging on the knob of the bolt.

"Middlun, Middlun," she called, "where on earth *are* you?"

"Holding the ladder for you, Mom," said a small voice beneath her.

Mom climbed down and looked sternly at her daughter.

"I was playing with the hammer, and it fit on the knob of the bolt, and then the bolt slid back. I didn't even have to push it."

"Why on earth didn't you tell Bigun?"

"He was doing such a good job of taking the window out. Besides, I don't especially like ladders, and he does. The only thing is, Mom, the bolt works now, but the hammer is sort of stuck to it."

"Then it can stay stuck," said Mom firmly, "just in case there's a next time."

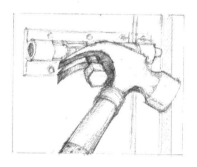

SPACESTRIDERS

Middlun suddenly wouldn't go near the bathroom. She cried going up the stairs, whimpered as she crept past it, and screamed bloody murder if anyone tried to wash her hair or make her take a bath.

"Whatever is the matter with you all of a sudden?" asked Mom. "You always liked baths, and you've got to brush your teeth and go to the bathroom sometime."

But Middlun only sobbed.

"I think it's the Spacestriders," said Bigun casually.

"What on earth are Spacestriders?" Mom looked really puzzled.

"They watch me," Middlun whispered.

*Middlun suddenly wouldn't
go near the bathroom.*

"Oh, for goodness' sake! Is it something on television, Bigun, puppets or a space cartoon or something?"

Bigun shrugged his shoulders.

"Not that I know of. She used to get pretty scared of the Mysterons and things like that, but it was usually the spooky music that got her. I've never heard of these Spacestriders, but she's always talking about them."

Mom put Middlun on her knee and said, "I've never heard of them either. Tell me about them, Middlun."

Middlun started to shake. Her mouth turned down at the edges, and her lips wobbled around so much she could hardly talk.

"They're in the b-b-b-bathroom, and they w-w-w-watch me," she wailed.

Bigun was just going to say, "Stupid," but Mom gave him a warning look, so he didn't. He just thought it instead.

"But what do they look like, Middlun?"

asked Mom gently, wrapping her arms right around her.

"They're j-j-just eyes. Big p-p-p-purple eyes," and Middlun squeezed her own eyes tightly shut at the horror of it all.

"But what do they *do*? Have they got hands and feet?" persisted Mom.

"N-no, just eyes. B-b-big ones. They're searching for me."

"They don't actually *do* anything," said Bigun in a lordly way, "so I don't really see what she's scared of. Actually it must be pretty boring for them if all they do is watch her. I mean, who wants to watch Middlun brushing her teeth or washing her face? Dead boring. And that's all they do."

"Well, it's funny that I've never seen them, and I'm sure Dad hasn't or he'd have told me. Or Littlun. I'm often in the bathroom with Littlun."

"But they're not watching out for *you*! It's

horrible!"

"Middlun, it's probably just a reflection of something in the tiles or the mirror. There aren't any such things as Spacestriders really. You're making a mistake."

"I'm not, I'm not," Middlun sobbed.

"Well, we'll go and look together, and if I can find them, I'll tell them a thing or two, frightening my poor little Middlun. Where do you usually see them?"

"Sometimes behind the toilet," Middlun almost croaked, trembling again, "and sometimes they're hiding behind the toothbrushes, and once they were behind the shower thing."

Mom got up, with Middlun clinging to her like a little monkey. "All right, we'll soon sort out these Spacestriders for you," and she marched to the bathroom and flung open the door.

"There, Middlun, I can't see any. They're not behind the toilet, or hiding behind the toothbrushes, or lurking in the shower curtain. And they're not under the towels or—oh, for goodness' sake, Middlun, open your eyes and help me look."

Middlun reluctantly opened one eye and shook her head. "They're not here now."

"There you are, you see. I told you there were no such things. And I'm old enough to know!" Mom laughed.

"They only come when it's dark," whispered Middlun nervously.

That night she woke Mom and Dad and Littlun with her screams. Dad picked her up and cuddled her.

"It's all right, Middlun, you were just having a nightmare. A nasty dream. What was it, Bigun pushing you over?"

"Worse."

"What, Littlun being sick all over you?"

"Much worse."

"Well, I can't think of anything much

Dad cuddled her. "It's all right,
you were just having a nightmare."

worse than that."

"It was Them. They were watching me."

Mom said, "Was it those 'thinks' again, Middlun, those spacewalkers?"

"Spacestriders. Only they're not 'thinks,' they're real."

"You've lost me now," said Dad. "What on earth are you talking about?" So Mom told him, and Dad laughed.

"As if I'd let anything nasty get into our bathroom, Middlun. It's just not allowed."

"You can't stop them," whispered Middlun. "They slide in through the gaps around the windows."

"And this only happens at night?"

"Yes, when you're not looking."

"Well, that's easy then. We'll leave the bathroom light on, and they won't know it's nighttime," he said cheerfully.

Middlun didn't look particularly cheered but allowed herself to be put back to bed. The next day she wouldn't go near the bathroom, and that night her screaming woke everyone up, even Bigun. Dad began to look angry. Bigun became irritable, and Mom was upset. Even after they had succeeded in getting the bigger ones back to bed, it took almost an hour of nursery rhymes and songs to get Littlun back to sleep. He thought the middle of the night was morning, and he wanted to play and have breakfast and watch the exercise lady puffing and waving her arms around on morning TV.

The next day Mom went out shopping by herself. When she came back, she called Middlun and sat her on her knee.

"Dad gave me a good idea last night. You know you said they only come at night?"

"Yes."

"Have you ever seen them in the bathroom in the daytime?"

"No."

"Or anywhere where it's light? Out in the garden in the sunshine, for instance?"

Middlun shook her head.

"Then I'm right," Mom said triumphantly. "Their eyes can't bear the light shining on them. It probably hurts them, so they have to go right away. Well, I went to a store and talked to a man about the Spacestriders, and he said he knew the answer. It's in here." And she handed Middlun a small package she had been hiding. Middlun took it eagerly. Even if she was terrified of Spacestriders, she liked packages.

"Oh, it's a flashlight," she said as she unwrapped the shiny green paper.

"Yes, and a very special one. It says 'Super Galactic Space-Beam' on it. If you can't remember that, ask Bigun to read it to you. Now, a Space-Beam is just what Spacestriders can't bear. It frightens them off like nothing else. The red cord on the handle goes loosely

46

"Oh, it's a flashlight," Middlun said
as she unwrapped the shiny green paper.

around your wrist at night, so you can't lose it in bed. And every time you see a Spacestrider, you shine the flashlight straight at it and say, 'Pow!' You won't see them again, I promise you. Oh, I do hope lots come. They're going to get such a fright, they'll never come here again! Let's have a little practice, shall we? Only remember, as you click the flashlight on, say 'Pow!' really loudly."

"Pow," said Middlun in a tiny voice.

"Oh, come *on*. Pretend you're shouting at Bigun."

"POW!" yelled Middlun, and grinned.

"Well, I'm deafened, so I hate to think what it will do to them."

They all had a good night's sleep that night, though Dad had expected to be woken by "pows" every five minutes.

The next morning Middlun gave the flashlight back to Mom.

"I won't be needing this anymore."

"Oh, I *am* glad to hear that! It worked then?"

"Sort of. They're watching Bigun now, instead of me."

Mom looked anxiously at Bigun, who was happily eating cereal.

"It doesn't bother me, Mom. I know how to handle them without a flashlight."

"Oh?"

"When they start watching, I twiddle my thumbs around and around like this"—he put his spoon down to demonstrate—"and they go cross-eyed trying to watch and get such dreadful headaches they go away. I'll teach you how to do it, Middlun, if you like. You get quicker with practice."

So Bigun showed Middlun how to do it, and Middlun showed Mom how to do it, and when Dad came in for breakfast, no one even looked up. They were all sitting around the table in total silence, and they were all twid-

Mom said, "It's supposed to give
Spacestriders blinding headaches."

dling their thumbs. Except for Littlun, who was still trying to knit his fingers together.

Dad listened to the silence, watching them in amazement.

"What's this, a prayer meeting?"

"No," said Mom, "it's supposed to give Spacestriders blinding headaches."

"I'm not surprised," said Dad, and showed Littlun how to do it too.

"If a Spacestrider came in now," said Mom, "and saw all five of us sitting here like this, concentrating on twiddling, *I* think it would die laughing."

"Better way to die than of blinding headaches," said Middlun.

*Dad was getting ready to open
the restaurant for lunch.*

ORPHANS

It was Saturday. Mom had gone off to her sister's for the day. Auntie Eileen was moving, and Mom had gone to help her. Dad was getting ready to open the restaurant for lunch. Meanwhile, Bigun was in charge.

As he went downstairs, Dad said, "You can stay up here in the apartment or play in the hall or even outside as long as you remember to stay on the tiles. Just be sensible and careful, and as long as I can see you or hear you, then I'll know you're all right. If you do go outside, make sure you wedge the front door open with the mat, Bigun. I don't want you trailing through the restaurant to get in again. And don't let Littlun anywhere near the curb—keep his reins on."

"I know all that," said Bigun.

"All right," said Dad. "Anyway, it's only till after the lunchtime rush. Then I'll shut the restaurant, and we'll do something nice in the afternoon."

For a while, the children played racetracks in the hall with Bigun's small cars. Then they went outside. It was a lovely sunny morning, with a fresh breeze blowing the colored tissue paper off the apples outside the fruit market. The front door banged behind them.

Bigun looked at Middlun.

"You should have held it," he said reproachfully. "Now we'll have to get back in through the restaurant, and Dad'll be mad."

"I was holding Littlun. He needs two hands. You should have gotten the mat ready."

"I was just going to. Anyway, we can always stay out here till Dad's finished."

All the stores on the block were set back from the sidewalk with an area of tiles outside, and the children were forbidden to play off the tiles. Middlun expertly clipped Littlun's reins around the lamppost. Littlun was quite happy with this arrangement. He could stand up for hours if he had something to hold on to, and there was always plenty to look at out on the tiles.

"All right, you choose now. What'll we play?" Bigun had chosen the racetrack game, so now it was his sister's turn.

"Orphans," said Middlun decidedly.

"Why do you always choose to play disasters, with poor little lost children being shipwrecked or trapped in some horrible castle or dying in a dungeon?"

"Because when we're finished playing, it's such a relief *not* to be lost in a dark jungle," said Middlun happily, "and to go and have a snack and watch TV. Your games make everyone feel much worse afterward. You and your friends always play being emperors with chariots, bossing everyone around, or Superman knocking skyscrapers over. When you're finished, it must feel awful to find that you're only Bigun after all, who has to be in bed by seven-thirty."

"O.K., it's orphans," said Bigun shortly. "What do you do?"

"Well, first you sit on the step and you feel miserable."

They both sat down on the edge of the tiles and looked sad.

"We've just run away from a horrible huge orphanage because the man who runs it is cruel and starves us. I saw him on TV and he was really *awful*. He chased people who ran away."

"All right," said Bigun, arranging a woeful expression on his face and letting his shoulders sag dejectedly. "Only we can run much faster than him, so he's miles away, tired out but still searching."

"Yes, and we don't have any money, and we haven't had anything to eat for days and days. Could we take our shoes off? We shouldn't really have shoes. Our feet should be all dirty and bleeding."

"No, Mom wouldn't like it," said Bigun. "And I wouldn't like the bleeding part. You might cut yourself if there's anything sharp on the ground."

They sucked their cheeks in and began to feel starving. Littlun watched them from his lamppost. They looked so dejected that his mouth began to turn down too.

"We should have a locket or something," Middlun said suddenly. "Orphans always do, and there's special writing inside, or a picture, and one day a kind old million-aire or something sees it, and remembers that it belonged to his dead daughter. And that's how he knows they're his long-lost grandchildren, and he takes them back to his house, which is always a mansion, and gives them horses and things." She jumped up excitedly and searched the sidewalk, found a squashed milk-bottle top, and joined Bigun again on the step. Bigun took it and stared at it with concentration.

"It's got a picture on it of an old-fashioned soldier with a beard. He was our dad, only we don't know it, and he got killed by a cannonball. Now, who's going to be the kind old millionaire who comes along and finds us?"

They both looked wistfully up and and down the sidewalk. Littlun's legs were beginning to ache, but it didn't occur to him to sit down.

"There's a lady there watching us," whispered Middlun uneasily, "but she's not a kind old anything. In fact, I think she's the wife of the nasty man at the orphanage, the one who only ever gave them gray soup to eat and made them work in the snow with no shoes on. She's still staring at us. Don't look at her, Bigun, and maybe she'll go away."

The woman, however, did not go away. She was tall and was wearing a hairy fur coat and thick purple stockings with wriggly patterns on them. Her feet were large, and her solid, sensible shoes made them look even larger.

Bigun and Middlun kept their heads down, but even so, they could see the purple wriggly patterns and the big shoes approaching.

Middlun cringed away from her, clutching Bigun, who was still holding the milk-bottle top in his cupped hands as if his life depended on it.

"Hello, children," said the fur coat.

"It's Her," whispered Middlun in a stricken voice, prepared to fend off blows.

"Do you live near here?"

Bigun looked up sideways at her and answered reluctantly, "Very near."

"And where's your mommy, children?"

Bigun could see that his sister was getting ready to start talking about being orphans, so he answered quickly, "She's gone away on a train."

"I see," the woman said, in a self-satisfied voice. "And where's your daddy?"

"He's at work."

The woman bent forward from the waist, lowering her top half until her face was incredibly close to the children.

"Then who is looking after you?"

Middlun looked up, feeling a strong dislike for this nosy, furry, big-footed lady, but she answered politely enough. "Bigun's in charge. Him . . ." and she shoved her elbow toward her brother in case the woman misunderstood.

"But why aren't you at home?"

Bigun was beginning to get tired of this insistent, persistent person.

"And where's your mommy, children?" the woman said.
"She's gone away on a train," Bigun answered.

"Got locked out," he said shortly.

"I see," said the woman in a voice full of meaning. Then she added, "I think your little baby might need changing."

"He often does," agreed Middlun, "but he'll have to wait. He doesn't mind."

The woman straightened up, looked around, then jackknifed down again.

"Have you eaten?"

Bigun looked up. "You mean recently?"

The woman frowned. "Yes, recently."

Bigun considered. They had had breakfast earlier than usual, because of taking Mom to the station.

"No, not recently," he decided.

"Are you hungry?"

"Starving," both children said in unison.

The woman thought for a few seconds, then seemed to make up her mind. She went into the burger restaurant, where there was a pay phone near the window.

"May I use your phone?" she asked the children's father.

"Help yourself," he answered, and went through the doors at the back to get some more lettuce from the fridge.

The woman dialed 911 and talked briefly but thoroughly. She was replacing the receiver as Dad returned with the lettuce, crisp and clean in a bowl, and another bowl of freshly sliced cucumber.

"Do you have a phone book?" she asked Dad imperiously. "Or do you happen to know the number of the local NCCAFA?"

"I'll get it for you," Dad said obligingly, "the book, I mean. I can't leave it out because it gets vandalized."

Just then, a group of boys shouldered their way into the restaurant. Some went straight to the counter, pushing each other, and some went to the Space Invaders machine. Dad handed the woman the phone book, glanced

63

out of the window to see that the children were still visible and not getting into mischief, and began to take orders.

The boys argued about who was having what, changed their orders twice, asked for change for the machine, and then complained it wasn't working properly.

"Sounds all right to me," said Dad, listening to the electronic bleeps and familiar high-pitched buzzes, then turned his back on all the noise and slapped burgers onto the griddles.

The police car stopped on the double-yellow lines outside Biggerburger, and a very pretty policewoman got out of the passenger seat and walked over to Littlun, looking at his reins.

The fur-coat lady, who had finished her second phone call, ran out as soon as she saw the police car and rushed at the policeman who had been driving.

The boys in the restaurant stopped kicking

the Space Invaders machine and formed a fairly orderly line, counting their money and arranging it in neat piles on the counter.

The woman in the fur coat was babbling at the policeman, "Babe in arms. Wanton neglect. You read about it all the time." And the policeman was saying pacifyingly, "Well, they look all right to me, but we'll soon get it sorted out. You can leave it to us now, madam; we've got your name and address, haven't we?"

Middlun was saying to the policewoman, "Don't take his reins off, or he'll go in the road. He likes lampposts, and he's practicing standing."

Bigun was saying, more or less to himself, "If you're not unloading or loading, I don't think you're allowed to stop on double-yellow lines."

Another car drew up behind the police car, and the fur-coat lady, obviously feeling

The woman in the fur coat was babbling at
the policeman, "Babe in arms. Wanton neglect."

dismissed by the policeman, ran over to it and banged on the window.

"If you are who I think you are, we're all here," she called importantly. A very discreet lady and gentleman emerged quietly from the car and tried to see what was going on.

The gang of boys left the restaurant and walked away quickly, burying their faces unnecessarily in the wrapping paper around their burgers. Dad glanced out of the window again to check the children, and came running out.

He counted first. All three were there, present and correct. He sighed with relief.

"What's happening? Bigun, what's going on? Here, I'll take Littlun. He looks as if he needs changing."

Slowly the fur-coat lady's face turned dark red, like a grape-juice stain spreading over a white bib. Then she looked hard at Middlun.

"Why didn't you tell me?" she asked, through closed teeth.

"What's happening? Bigun,
what's going on?" said Dad.

"You didn't ask. Anyway, we're not really allowed to talk to strangers, and you did ask a lot of questions."

It ended up with a party in the apartment. It was only a short one, but there were burgers all around as it was lunchtime, and cups of tea that the policeman and the nice quiet lady from the NCCAFA made, with Middlun telling them where everything was kept. It was great fun.

The only person who wasn't invited was the fur-coat lady, but the policeman had thanked her and said she was public-spirited. The man from the NCCAFA had thanked her too, and said that it *might* have been a real case, so it was better to be on the safe side. So she went off, feeling virtuous but a little foolish. At times like this, she really wasn't at all sure that she liked children. Not at all sure.

Everybody jumped when Dad
suddenly yelled, "Wow!"

LITTLE
ORANGE

The family was sitting around the table having breakfast. Mom was helping Littlun to feed himself, and Dad was opening letters. Four brown envelopes today and one green one. The brown ones were all bills, which Dad didn't like opening, but he started with those and saved the green one till last. Bigun was reading the back of a cereal box, and Middlun was spooning Wheat Chex into her mouth one at a time, pretending each one was a package she was sending, with something nice inside. They were all being quiet because of the bills, so everybody jumped when Dad suddenly yelled, "Wow!"

Everybody sat up and looked at him. He

was reading the green letter. It was from two very special friends of the family who were going abroad for a year, and they were offering Mom and Dad their beach house while they were away. In the bottom of the envelope jingled some keys with "Cockleshell" written on a label.

"Oh, my goodness," breathed Mom. "Oh, how marvelous! Isn't it kind of them?"

Dad handed her the letter and as she read it, she couldn't stop smiling.

"It's got four beds and a little kitchen. The front windows face the harbor, and the sea is beyond some dunes just behind it. There's a little store and a beach café open for the summer season, and it's even got a boat. Oh, it does sound lovely, and it's not too far away!"

"When can we go there?" asked Bigun.

"The next fine Sunday," said Dad, "and we'll stay the night."

It was impossible for the family to go away

for a really long vacation because of the burger restaurant having to be open. But it was always closed on Sundays and Mondays, so they could go to the beach house for two days as often as they could manage.

Then Middlun said, "But Bigun has school on Mondays. He can't go."

Bigun glared at her. He'd already thought of that.

"Don't be nasty, Middlun," said Mom. "An occasional day off never hurt anybody. I'll ask his teacher next time I see her."

So the children began to take an intense interest in the weather forecasts, and Mom began to make lists. She was good at lists, having had lots of practice, and made them for everything. She said it kept her mind in order, and it certainly meant she forgot things less often than most people.

Then one Saturday it was fine all day, and the forecaster on television cautiously suggested that Sunday might be warmer too, apart from mist on the south coast, which would soon clear.

"Right," said Dad to Middlun, who was hovering hopefully by the restaurant door. "Tell Mom it's on. We'll go early tomorrow morning and see Cockleshell for ourselves!"

So Mom found her lists, and Bigun dug out four knapsacks, big ones for Mom and Dad and smaller ones for himself and Middlun. Littlun was too small to have a knapsack of his own, so his things had to be tucked into all the others.

They took thick sweaters in case it was cold, jackets in case it was wet, and shorts in case it was hot. And candles in case the gas tanks were empty, and matches in case there were none already there. And packages of soup and cookies, and bread and butter and milk and jam, because the store would not be open yet. Books went in, and puppets, and hot-water

*Bigun dug out four knapsacks, big ones for Mom
and Dad and smaller ones for himself and Middlun.*

bottles and diapers, and Littlun's favorite dog with floppy ears. The knapsacks were bulging by this time, but Mom still stuffed in extra towels, pillowcases, and an extra dish towel, plastic bags for trash, and just a few cleaning things.

"For goodness' sake, let's get everything into the van quickly, Bigun, before we need to rent a trailer," Dad said, after he had closed the restaurant. So they loaded everything into the van, ready for an early start the next morning.

The sun shone brightly as they left. Middlun had found some plastic sunglasses from last year, and soon it was so hot that Mom and Dad rolled the windows down. They sang songs in the van, very loudly, and Dad put in different words, which made them all laugh.

Mom had a map, and just after she had said, "We're about halfway there now," the sun disappeared, hidden in thick mist.

"Oh, well," said Mom, "we know we're getting near the coast, because that's what the forecaster said. It'll soon go away."

But it didn't. It got worse. Middlun's sunglasses came off, coats were put back on, and they had to roll up the windows because the wind was so icy. All the cars were going more slowly now, and many of them had their headlights on.

"We'll go to the wharf and take the boat," said Dad. "It'll be much quicker than going all the way around the harbor and catching the minitrain."

It took a long time to find the wharf. Bigun could tell Mom was lost because she kept turning the map around and around, but at last they arrived and parked near the harbor mouth. They could not actually see the sea because of the fog, but they could hear seagulls squabbling nearby. Dad opened his door and said, "Wait here, and I'll find out when the ferry goes."

It was extraordinarily quiet, once the gulls had stopped arguing. Nobody was around, and there were no other cars. Nearby shops were so thoroughly boarded up for the winter, they looked as if they would never open again. Middlun said, "It's a little spooky, isn't it, and what's that funny noise?"

They all listened as a strange "hoo-hoo" noise filtered through the fog, sometimes faintly and then sounding oddly near.

"It's only a foghorn," said Mom brightly, "warning boats they're near land. Let's time it."

"Here's Dad," said Bigun, as he heard foot-steps. "Oh, no it isn't. It's just a lady walking her dog. He's been gone a long time, hasn't he?"

Mom jumped out of the van and stopped the woman.

"Can you tell me when the ferry runs,

please, over to the beach houses?"

"Oh, dear, you're much too early," the woman laughed boisterously. "You'll have to come back at Easter! The season only starts at Easter, you know, then everything opens up." Suddenly she bellowed into the mists.

"Charger, Charger! Now, where's that hound of mine raced off to?"

Mom pointed to the woman's efficient-looking shoes, where a bedraggled Yorkshire terrier crouched, damp and despairing.

"Having a rest, are you? He does enjoy his brisk walks. He hauls me out every day, rain or shine. Doesn't seem to feel the cold." And the lady strode away, with the wispy little dog drooping behind her. They both disappeared into the fog just as Dad loomed up.

"Nothing doing," Dad and Mom told each other at exactly the same time, and jumped into the van, blowing on their hands to warm them up. "We'll go around the harbor and find the train," said Dad.

Eventually they came to the parking lot, café, and tiny station. It was utterly deserted, and the ticket office was closed. They were all cold by now, and Dad looked at Mom.

"Back home or on?"

"How far is it?"

"Well, the train takes you the first mile and a half, and then it's about half a mile along the beach to the house. It's not really so far. It's just cold and damp. We could load the children's knapsacks onto the stroller, and I'll carry Littlun."

"Except the one thing I forgot to bring is the stroller," said Mom miserably. "It was on my list, but . . ."

A shout of laughter came from nowhere. It was really weird. They all looked at each other. Then Dad walked to a door in the café building, and knocked loudly. There was no window on that side and no handle on the door, yet it opened. Inside, three men were crouched by an electric stove, burning toast and laughing. The heat from the little room rolled out toward the family, engulfing them in a wave of warmth.

The men were so nice, once they understood that the train was needed, and invited the family in to huddle near the fire. Then one of the men disappeared into a nearby shed and came back driving a little wooden engine with two wooden carriages behind.

"Are you *sure* you want to go to the houses? Nobody else does, not in this weather. We haven't had any passengers for days."

"Yes, please," said Dad. "We're staying overnight."

The men laughed.

" 'Course I'll take you, but you'll find it's pretty cold. And there's no electricity."

"We've got candles," said Mom, rather faintly. Then she brightened up a little. "And

*One of them came back driving a little wooden
engine with two wooden carriages behind.*

hot-water bottles."

He drove them downhill toward the harbor through a nature preserve of dripping trees. They couldn't see the sea at all until they were actually at the beach. As they unloaded, the driver said, "Look, I'll come down again at four o'clock and wait five minutes. If you change your minds about staying, just be here and I'll take you back. Long walk, otherwise, with the children."

"Thanks. It should be all right, but we'll be here at four o'clock if it isn't."

The train looped around a shelter and was sucked into the fog.

The family adjusted their knapsacks, and Dad carried Littlun. There was a wobbly line of beach houses on the sandy edge of the harbor.

"Bigun and Middlun, you go on ahead. It's the only orange one, and it's called Cockleshell. Find it!"

It was bitterly cold, with an icy, penetrating dampness that reddened their noses. Dad unzipped his big jacket and tucked Littlun inside. Littlun obviously liked it, just his face sticking out.

"You look pregnant," laughed Mom. "Now you know what it feels like with that bump in front! Hey, look at all the driftwood. If there's no heat, we could build a fire in the dunes."

"I already thought of that," said Dad. "Most of the wood at the high-water mark is pretty wet, but there seems to be drier stuff blown nearer the houses. Must have been the gales. Don't worry, we'll get warm somehow."

There was a distant shriek, and two little lumpy figures wobbled out of the fog toward them.

"We've found it! We've found it! And it's lovely."

Two little lumpy figures
wobbled out of the fog toward them.

They stumbled on over the sand, and there it was—the only one that was painted a sunshiny-orange, the only one with a little bay window facing the harbor. The water lapped up to about two yards away from the window.

Dad found the keys and opened the door at the back. They all held their breath. The house was only about the size of a garage, but a little longer and maybe a little narrower.

"It's like a boat," breathed Middlun, "pointing out to sea."

Mom headed straight for the little kitchen in the middle of the house.

"Gas works," she cried delightedly, and lit the oven with a match from a large box nearby. "And the matches aren't even damp! We'll be warm in no time at all." With the oven door open to let out the heat, she rummaged in her knapsack and found two cans of soup. The first drawer she opened produced a canopener, and the first cabinet she tried held a nest of pans. Dad discovered a folding table, and within about five minutes they were all drinking mugs of hot tomato soup.

"These bench seats we're sitting on pull out to make a large bed, and you three will be in the bunk beds near the door. Bigun on top this time, and Middlun and Littlun can share the bottom one. After lunch, we'll get all the bedding out and make hot-water bottles to warm it up," said Mom happily.

"We'll go and fill the water container, Bigun, as soon as we've had our soup," Dad said. "There are supposed to be taps outside, if they haven't all been turned off for the winter." Mom looked at him with horror.

"If there's no fresh water, that's it. I hadn't thought it might be turned off. We've only got some milk and two more cans of soup. The rest are all packages, and everything needs water."

Dad and Bigun disappeared with the water

container, while Mom soaked bread in soup and spooned it into Littlun. Middlun made a thorough search of everything, calling out as she went.

"More pans and bowls in here, Mom, and a bucket and cleaning stuff. Towels and spare sheets in this drawer, Mom. Look, there are flashlights in this one, and they work. And candles and more matches. And writing paper and pens, and a pack of cards. Oh, and dominoes and . . ."

"They've got everything," said Mom. "Why on earth did I pack all that stuff?"

"Can't we leave it here?" asked Middlun, who didn't want to carry it all back again.

Dad and Bigun clumped in through the door, staggering with a full container of fresh water.

"We found the Beach Office. There's a phone booth behind it, and the rest rooms, open and working. The fresh-water tap is just

Dad and Bigun clumped in through the door,
staggering with a full container of fresh water.

outside."

"Now we've got everything," said Mom comfortably.

"Poor Mr. Train-driver," cried Middlun suddenly. "I hope he doesn't wait too long."

While Littlun had a nap, Bigun helped Mom make up the beds and tuck hot-water bottles in, and put away everything they had brought with them. Dad and Middlun crossed the dunes to find the sea. Then they came back to fetch the others, and Littlun was tucked into Dad's jacket again.

Middlun was full of information. "We've found where the ferry comes from, and you can just see the wharf where we first parked. Some of the beach houses are really fancy, and one even has a television, because it's got an antenna at the side." Mom shuddered. "But we like Little Orange best."

They walked along, enjoying the spooky loneliness of the place, the deserted dunes, tufted with bleached and brittle knife-grass, the closed-up houses, and the upturned boats lying on the sand. Then they went back to the hut and lit candles and played cards and dominoes around the table. The little oven had warmed the hut so well that they turned it off and had supper cozily by candlelight.

The next morning the fog had been blown away by fierce winds. Even the harbor water was in a state of uproar, and the few fishing boats moored to round plastic buoys tugged and bounced like little dogs pulling at a new lead. Waves crashed and pounded on the shore, churning the pebbles with a growling noise and flinging spray over the dunes. They could see the wharf clearly now, across the narrow harbor mouth, with high seas flooding right over the parking lot.

"No wonder the ferry isn't running yet," said Dad.

Reluctantly, they cleaned the house and

Bigun said, "My boots are full of sand,
and so are my socks, and so's my hair . . ."

packed everything away to leave it tidy for next time. It was easier going back with empty knapsacks, and the train was there, specially waiting for them.

As they were driving home, Dad said, "If it was as good as that in fog and gales, what will it be like in summer?"

"Wasn't it lovely?" Mom sighed. "Just to read by candlelight, and to go to bed early, and have no phone and no TV?"

Bigun said, "My boots are full of sand, and so are my socks, and so's my hair, and my ears, and all my pockets."

"My face feels all tight and stretched, and my hair tastes lovely," said Middlun, and she sucked the end of her braid all the way home.

Littlun didn't say anything. He always went to sleep in the van anyway. But this time, he went to sleep smiling.

When Middlun ran out of paper,
she drew on the fridge door.

ANGELS ON
ROLLER SKATES

Middlun had suddenly discovered how to draw angels. She drew a person first, and then she drew a tall triangle on each shoulder. She was amazed. All her people now had wings, and all of them were angels. She drew and drew and drew. When she ran out of paper, she drew on the fridge door. Mom wasn't pleased, because that sort of red marker doesn't come off very well, and it left pink ghost angels all over the white enamel.

Then Middlun discovered that if she drew crisscross lines on her people's feet and two little circles underneath each foot, then all her people were wearing roller skates. She was ecstatic. Now all her angels were on roller skates! She drew them skating over hills and skating across bridges. She drew them skating up steps.

Bigun was scornful.

"You can't roller-skate *down* steps, you idiot."

"They're roller-skating *up* steps, Bigun. Can't you tell up from down?"

"It doesn't matter. You can't roller-skate up *or* down steps."

"Angels can," said Middlun. "That's the difference between us and them."

Mom was becoming frazzled by it all, but then Dad gave Middlun a whole roll of wallpaper so she could draw on the back of it. Middlun was almost delirious with joy. She rolled it along the landing floor and drew and drew and drew.

Angels with roller skates were riding on horses. Angels with roller skates were sitting on rooftops taking a rest. Angels with roller

*Middlun rolled the wallpaper along the landing
floor and drew and drew and drew.*

skates were having a wonderful picnic on the beach with a huge tablecloth spread out on the sand, and all Middlun's favorite food was drawn on little plates. There were chocolate cookies and banana sandwiches, a small piece of roast lamb in a great green sea of mint jelly, pink milk shakes and waffles, asparagus soup and cheese slices, and a very large dish of shrimp cocktail.

Bigun sat on the banisters and watched.

"I told you you were an idiot. If you roller-skated on the beach, you'd get sand in the ball bearings. Then they wouldn't work at all."

"Bigun," Mom shouted from the kitchen, "why don't you stop being so critical? In any case, I don't think skates even have ball bearings these days."

"Well, mine do. Those skates you got me from Oxfam with the special little wrench to make them bigger. They keep leaking ball bearings all over the pavement. I'm always trying to scoop them up and pour them back."

Mom decided it was time to change the subject before Bigun suggested he needed a new pair with brakes and four-wheel drive. She knew how much *they* cost.

"Middlun, would you stop drawing now, because it's almost supper time, and I want to wash your hair afterward. Don't you remember what's happening tomorrow?" Middlun finished drawing an enormous cake, big enough for all the angels at the picnic to share, and reluctantly began to roll up the paper.

"Yes, I'm going to school." She looked at Bigun, hoping that he would fall off the banisters in surprise. Or at least look impressed. He did neither.

"How boring," was all he said, and he wandered off to watch the weather forecast until supper was ready.

Middlun was starting school for real next term, but all the new children had been invited to school for a morning to meet the teachers and find out what they would be doing in class. A parent had to come too, in case.

"In case what?" Middlun asked.

"In case you're scared. Of a new place or lots of big children. Anything," said Mom. But Middlun was not scared. She was looking forward to it. It was Mom who was nervous. And Bigun. He was always worrying.

"You don't go in our door, Mom. You use the green one around the side. And Mrs. Mitchell's got shaggy hair and green glasses. You can't miss her. Can Middlun read her own name? 'Cause she'll have to, to find her peg. They don't use pictures except in the nursery. And are all her clothes named? Or she'll lose them sure as anything. Mrs. Mitchell gets mad if clothes aren't named."

"For goodness' sake, Bigun, that's why we're going tomorrow. In any case, it's not so long ago that I was taking *you* for the first time, remember? I don't suppose everything has changed since then. Stop worrying, Middlun."

But Middlun wasn't in the least worried. She was remembering not to forget to draw some lemon cheesecake for the angels' picnic on the beach. She thought angels would like it.

Mom and Middlun arrived at school the next morning and remembered to use the side door. Mrs. Mitchell sat all the new children around an orange table and gave them scissors and paste and lots of magazines to cut up and make into sticky pictures. Then she talked quietly to the parents.

The children at all the other tables were being very good. But while their hands were busy doing things, their eyes were watching the new ones. The little boy next to Middlun couldn't make his scissors work, so he started crying. His dad dropped the information

101

*The little boy next to Middlun couldn't make
his scissors work, so he started crying.*

sheets Mrs. Mitchell was giving him and rushed to pick him up.

Middlun looked around the room with interest. One group was coiling pots out of PlayDoh. Mom wouldn't let her have Play-Doh at home because Bigun had squidged some into the carpet. Middlun picked up her chair and squeezed herself in at the coiled pot table.

"Hello, friends," she said cheerfully. "Can I play?" She took a chunk of purple PlayDoh from a little girl with pale hair and started rolling a long snake. The little girl decided that she didn't want purple anyway and took some green to make a handle for her pot.

Mom knew it was time to go. Middlun was happy, but if there was going to be a rumpus about her being at the wrong table, Mom was sure Mrs. Mitchell would handle it better if she wasn't there.

"See you later then." She waved as she went

103

out, but Middlun wasn't looking. Her snake now stretched almost to the end of the table, and the little girl with pale hair was showing her how to make a pot with it.

When Mom came back at lunchtime to collect her, all the other children were clutching sticky pictures, and windmills made out of toilet paper rolls and wooden lollipop sticks. Middlun had nothing to take home. Mrs. Mitchell explained.

"The big table was doing a poster competition for the Children's Hospital. The best picture from this area will win a prize. Middlun really wanted to do one too, after she had finished her PlayDoh. I couldn't stop her. I suppose it's all right to send it in with the others, because by the time they do the judging she will be a member of the school."

Mom laughed. "Please don't worry about sending it in. I'm sure Middlun won't mind."

Middlun glared at her.

"I will. It's a very good picture." Before Mom had time to say anything, Mrs. Mitchell sent Middlun off to find her coat and whispered, "It *is* amazingly good. Most original. They were supposed to do something about hospitals, and most of them, of course, painted pictures of children with spots or sitting up in bed all bandaged up. Your daughter painted a nurse with angel's wings. And do you know, the nurse was on roller skates! Now isn't that unusual? I think it stands a very good chance."

When they got home, Mom told Dad and Bigun all about Middlun's introduction to school and the poster competition.

"I suppose Middlun did an angel on roller skates?" Dad sighed.

"Of course I did," said Middlun. "Only I put her in a blue striped dress with a white cap and apron and a big red cross on the cap to show she was a nurse. And I put in one of those little upside-down watches they wear on their aprons too."

"What's the prize?" asked Bigun. But they had forgotten to ask.

A few weeks later they found out Middlun had won the prize, and her picture was going to be used as a huge poster all over the area. She was invited to the Children's Hospital with her family and Mrs. Mitchell for the presentation. Cameras clicked and everybody clapped while she opened the box. Only Mrs. Mitchell guessed what might be in it. And she was right. Inside was a brand-new pair of the most beautiful roller skates you've ever seen.

T H E

END